GOOD JOB, OLIVER!

Laurel Molk

Crown Publishers, Inc.
New York

For Jack Andrew and Coco
with all my love

and with love to Ilana and Sandy

Published by Crown Publishers, Inc., a Random House company,
201 East 50th Street, New York, NY 10022

CROWN is a trademark of Crown Publishers, Inc.

www.randomhouse.com/kids/

Library of Congress Cataloging-in-Publication Data
Molk, Laurel.
Good job, Oliver! / written and illustrated by Laurel Molk.
p. cm.
Summary: Oliver Bunny sets out to prove to the big bunnies that he can win
the annual strawberry contest, but he is still his mother's little bunny boy.
[1. Rabbits—Fiction. 2. Strawberries—Fiction.
3. Gardening—Fiction.] I.Title.
PZ7.M7334Go 1998
[E]—dc21 97-21265

ISBN 0-517-70975-9 (trade)
0-517-70976-7 (lib. bdg.)

Printed in Singapore

10 9 8 7 6 5 4 3 2 1

First Edition

Oliver bounced ahead of Mother Bunny on their way to the old oak tree. They were going to enter the annual strawberry contest. Oliver couldn't wait to grow the biggest and best strawberries ever!

Many bunnies were gathered under the oak tree. When Oliver got his seeds, the bigger bunnies teased him. The biggest bunny said, "*Little* bunnies grow *little* berries."

Oliver was angry. "They shouldn't tease me just because I'm little," he told his mother.

"No, they shouldn't," she agreed. "Go ahead and grow the best berries you can."

So Oliver planted his seeds near some sunflowers and blueberry bushes, far from the big bunnies' garden.

After just a few days, birds began to eat the seeds in the big bunnies' garden. But the big bunnies were ready!

They waved banners and blew horns. They chased the birds away.

Oliver watched and worried. Just one little bunny couldn't chase away all those birds. *Think, Oliver, think!* What do birds like better than strawberry seeds?

Oliver picked sunflowers and threw them on the ground. And
not a minute too soon. The birds swooped down and ate sunflower
seeds until they were too full to even think about strawberry seeds.
Good job, Oliver.

Days passed and the seeds grew into plants with tiny white flowers and green leaves. Oliver weeded and watered them every day.

Then one day gophers came to the big bunnies' garden patch.
But the big bunnies were ready! They pounded the ground and
banged on cymbals and were so noisy that the gophers ran away.

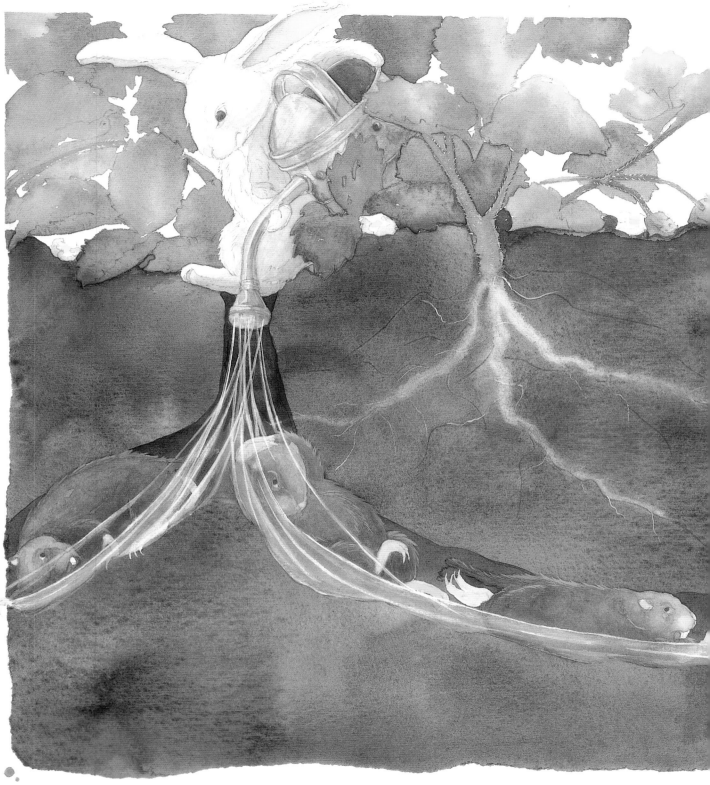

Oliver watched and worried. How much noise could one little bunny make? *Think, Oliver, think!*

Oliver grabbed the watering can and raced from hole to hole pouring water in.

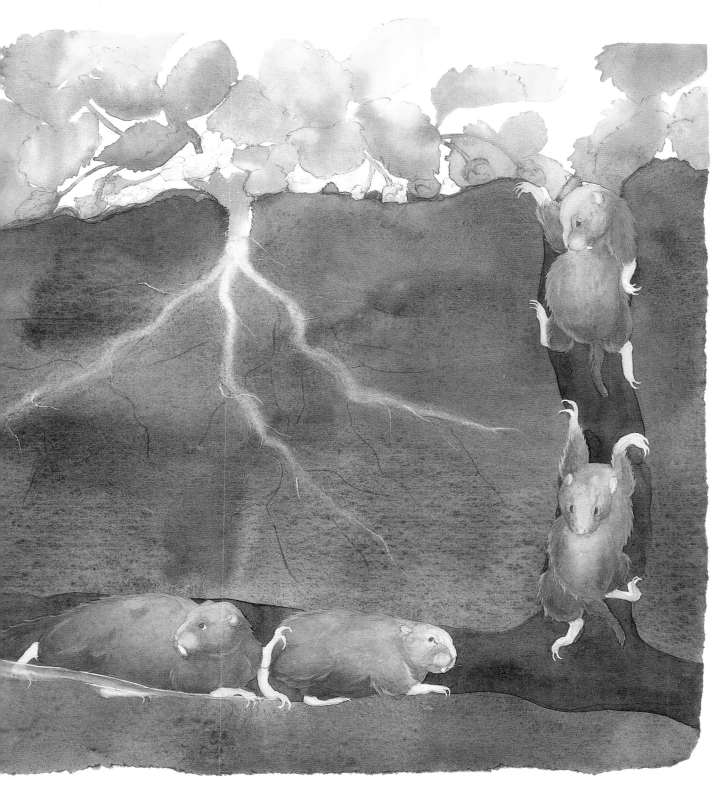

The gophers got so wet and cranky that they didn't even want
to think about strawberry plants.
Good job, Oliver.

STOMP!

With time and sun and rain, all of the plants were finally covered with big red strawberries. And then one day the ground shook.

STOMP!

STOMP!

STOMP!

Oh, no! Big hungry bears!
The big bunnies ran and hid. The bears gobbled up the big bunnies' delicious berries.

Oliver watched and worried. His mother had told him that he must run and hide if he saw a bear. What could a little bunny do? *Think, Oliver, think!*

Oliver threw pebbles and dirt into the empty watering can. Then he hid in the blueberry bushes.

STOMP!

STOMP!

STOMP!

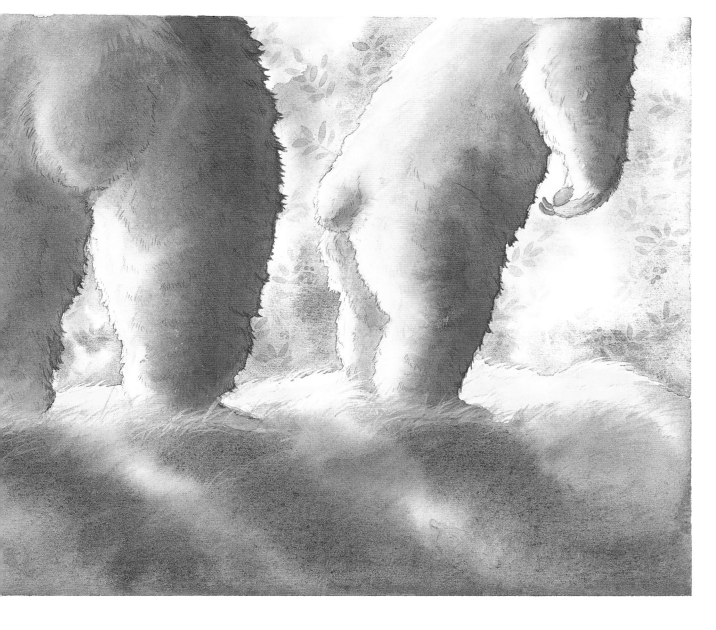

Oliver peeked out between the leaves and saw BIG hairy feet in front of his nose. He was scared, but he stayed hidden and shook his watering can.

RATTLE! RATTLE!

RATTLE!   The bears looked around.

"RATTLESNAKE!" a bear shouted.

Good job, Oliver.

Oliver jumped out of the bushes.
He saw his mother and ran to her.

"I am so proud of you, Oliver," she
told him. "Even though you are the
littlest bunny, you have grown the best
strawberries ever."

The big bunnies came out of hiding and gathered around Oliver. The biggest bunny said, "The littlest bunny grew the biggest berries.

"Oliver, you are one plucky bunny—*and* the winner of this year's contest!"

There were enough berries on Oliver's vines for everyone
to share. The bunnies made strawberry shortcake and
strawberry ice cream sundaes and strawberry cupcakes
and strawberry pie and strawberry jam.

Too soon, Mother Bunny called to Oliver, "It's bedtime, my bunny boy."

Oliver said, "Actually, I'm big enough to grow strawberries and win contests now and I don't need to go to bed."

Mother Bunny picked Oliver up and told him,
"You are a wonderful bunny and you grow wonderful
strawberries, but it is *still* your bedtime."

So Oliver snuggled up close to Mother Bunny and
fell asleep as she carried him home to bed.